Ar gyfer Jude. Gyda fy
nymuniadau gorau, diolch – J.L.

tiger tales
5 River Road, Suite 128, Wilton, CT 06897
Published in the United States 2019
Originally published in France 2018
by Piccolia
Text and illustrations copyright © 2018 Jonny Lambert
ISBN-13: 978-1-68010-129-4
ISBN-10: 1-68010-129-3
Printed in China
LTP/1400/2402/0818
10 9 8 7 6 5 4 3 2 1

For more insight and activities,
visit us at www.tigertalesbooks.com

THE BIG, ANGRY ROAR

by Jonny Lambert

tiger tales

As the pride patrolled,
the lion cubs squabbled.

First a push,

then a tumble,

followed by an "OW!"

"Stop it, you two!
Cub, don't hurt your
sister. You're old
enough to know better!"

"But she started it!"
snapped Cub.

And off he stomped.

"I'm so angry!" scowled Cub.
"I think I might burst!"

"Bursting won't help," giggled Gnu.
"And it's terribly messy!" Zebra
snickered. "Cub, you need to
learn how to let your
anger out."

"When we're angry, we **stamp**

and **STOMP!**"

Cub stamped and stomped up and down.

"Ouch! That hurt!" he angrily yelped.
"I stomped on a stone. Stomping doesn't work!"

Nursing a sore paw, Cub stormed off.
"I'm really angry now!" he shouted.
And he huffed and puffed and grumped!

"Oh, stop your huffing and puffing!" snorted Rhino.
"You should do what we do," said Hippo.
"When we're annoyed . . .

"...we

bash

and

crash,

splatter and splash!"

Cub charged up and down.
"Yuck! Now I'm smelly!" he cried.
"Crashing and splashing is silly!"

Sulking and stinky, Cub clomped on . . .

SMACK!

. . . right into Elephant's bottom.

"Hey, you're in my way!" shouted Cub.

"TOOT!" trumpeted Elephant angrily.

"ROAR!" growled Cub.

TOOT! TOOT!

ROAR!

ROAR!

And they started
a huge . . .

STA

MPEDE!

"Oh, no!" squeaked Cub.
"Did . . . did we do that?"
Baboon nodded.
He'd seen it all before.

"Everyone gets angry,"
smiled Baboon. "I do, too.
But I know how to let
the anger out. Let me show
you what to do.

"First, breathe deeply in
and out, and slowly
count to 10.

"Make a bunch of funny faces,

then start all over again!"

"I feel so much better," chuckled Cub, "and I'm not angry anymore. But I do have something important to say . . .

"I'm sorry."